6840400286 1 111

D1630847

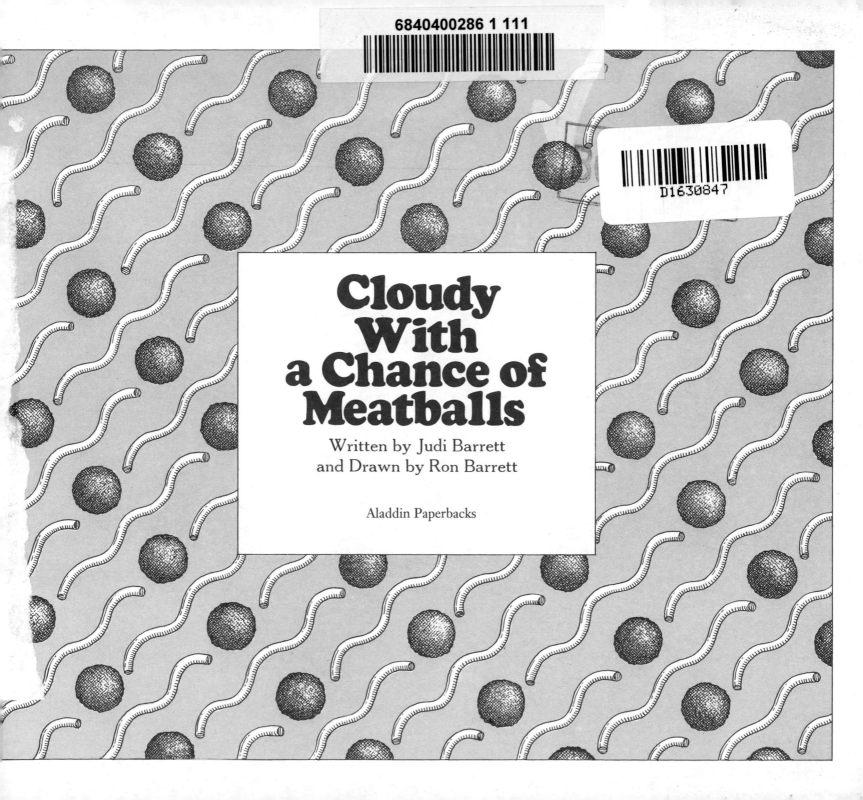

Cloudy With a Chance of Meatballs

Written by Judi Barrett
and Drawn by Ron Barrett

Aladdin Paperbacks

LEICESTER CITY LIBRARIES	
111	
Bertrams	17.05.08
PIC	£5.99

Library of Congress Cataloging-in-Publication Data

Barrett, Judi.
Cloudy with a chance of meatballs/written by Judi Barrett and
drawn by Ron Barrett.—1st Aladdin Books ed.
p. cm.
Summary: Life is delicious in the town of Chewandswallow where it
rains soup and juice, snows mashed potatoes, and blows storms of
hamburgers—until the weather takes a turn for the worse.
ISBN 0-689-70749-5 (pbk.)
[1. Weather—Fiction.   2. Food—Fiction.]   I. Barrett, Ron, ill.
II. Title.   87-29643
PZ7.B2752C1 1988   CIP
[E]—dc 19   AC

Aladdin Paperbacks
An imprint of Simon & Schuster
Children's Publishing Division
1230 Avenue of the Americas
New York, NY 10020
Text copyright © 1978 by Judi Barrett
Illustrations copyright © 1978 by Ron Barrett
All rights reserved including the right of reproduction
in whole or in part in any form.
First Aladdin Paperbacks edition, 1982
Also available in a hardcover edition from
Atheneum Books for Young Readers
Printed in the United States of America
49 50

We were all sitting around the big kitchen table. It was Saturday morning. Pancake morning. Mom was squeezing oranges for juice. Henry and I were betting on how many pancakes we each could eat. And Grandpa was doing the flipping.

Seconds later, something flew through the air headed toward the kitchen ceiling . . .

. . . and landed right on Henry.

After we realized that the flying object was only a pancake, we all laughed, even Grandpa. Breakfast continued quite uneventfully. All the other pancakes landed in the pan. And all of them were eaten, even the one that landed on Henry.

That night, touched off by the pancake incident at breakfast, Grandpa told us the best tall-tale bedtime story he'd ever told.

"Across an ocean, over lots of huge bumpy mountains, across three hot deserts, and one smaller ocean . . .

. . . there lay the tiny town of Chewandswallow.

In most ways, it was very much like any other tiny town. It had a Main Street lined with stores, houses with trees and gardens around them, a schoolhouse, about three hundred people, and some assorted cats and dogs.

But there were no food stores in the town of Chewandswallow. They didn't need any. The sky supplied all the food they could possibly want.

The only thing that was really different about Chewandswallow was its weather. It came three times a day, at breakfast, lunch, and dinner. Everything that everyone ate came from the sky.

Whatever the weather served, that was what they ate.

But it never rained rain. It never snowed snow. And it never blew just wind. It rained things like soup and juice. It snowed mashed potatoes and green peas. And sometimes the wind blew in storms of hamburgers.

The people could watch the weather report on television in the morning and they would even hear a prediction for the next day's food.

When the townspeople went outside, they carried their plates, cups, glasses, forks, spoons, knives and napkins with them. That way they would always be prepared for any kind of weather.

If there were leftovers, and there usually were, the people took them home and put them in their refrigerators in case they got hungry between meals.

The menu varied.

By the time they woke up in the morning, breakfast was coming down.

After a brief shower of orange juice, low clouds of sunny-side up eggs moved in followed by pieces of toast. Butter and jelly sprinkled down for the toast. And most of the time it rained milk afterwards.

For lunch one day, frankfurters, already in their rolls, blew in from the northwest at about five miles an hour.

There were mustard clouds nearby. Then the wind shifted to the east and brought in baked beans.

A drizzle of soda finished off the meal.

Dinner one night consisted of lamb chops, becoming heavy at times, with occasional ketchup. Periods of peas and baked potatoes were followed by gradual clearing, with a wonderful Jell-O setting in the west.

The Sanitation Department of Chewandswallow had a rather unusual job for a sanitation department. It had to remove the food that fell on the houses and sidewalks and lawns. The workers cleaned things up after every meal and fed all the dogs and cats. Then they emptied some of it into the surrounding oceans for the fish and turtles and whales to eat. The rest of the food was put back into the earth so that the soil would be richer for the people's flower gardens.

One day there was nothing but Gorgonzola cheese all day long.

The next day there was only broccoli, all overcooked.

And the next day there were brussel sprouts and peanut butter with mayonnaise.

Another day there was a pea soup fog. No one could see where they were going and they could barely find the rest of the meal that got stuck in the fog.

The food was getting larger and larger, and so were the portions. The people were getting frightened. Violent storms blew up frequently. Awful things were happening.

One Tuesday there was a hurricane of bread and rolls all day long and into the night. There were soft rolls and hard rolls, some with seeds and some without. There was white bread and rye and whole wheat toast. Most of it was larger than they had ever seen bread and rolls before. It was a terrible day. Everyone had to stay indoors. Roofs were damaged, and the Sanitation Department was beside itself. The mess took the workers four days to clean up, and the sea was full of floating rolls.

To help out, the people piled up as much bread as they could in their backyards. The birds picked at it a bit, but it just stayed there and got staler and staler.

There was a storm of pancakes one morning and a downpour of maple syrup that nearly flooded the town. A huge pancake covered the school. No one could get it off because of its weight, so they had to close the school.

Lunch one day brought fifteen-inch drifts of cream cheese and jelly sandwiches. Everyone ate themselves sick and the day ended with a stomachache.

There was an awful salt and pepper wind accompanied by an even worse tomato tornado. People were sneezing themselves silly and running to avoid the tomatoes. The town was a mess. There were seeds and pulp everywhere.

The Sanitation Department gave up. The job was too big.

Everyone feared for their lives. They couldn't go outside most of the time. Many houses had been badly damaged by giant meatballs, stores were boarded up and there was no more school for the children.

So a decision was made to abandon the town of Chewand-swallow.

It was a matter of survival.

. . took the absolute necessities with them, and set sail on their rafts for a new land.

After being afloat for a week, they finally reached a small coastal town, which welcomed them. The bread had held up surprisingly well, well enough for them to build temporary houses for themselves out of it.

The children began school again, and the adults all tried to find places for themselves in the new land. The biggest change they had to make was getting used to buying food at a supermarket. They found it odd that the food was kept on shelves, packaged in boxes, cans and bottles. Meat that had to be cooked was kept in large refrigerators. Nothing came down from the sky except rain and snow. The clouds above their heads were not made of fried eggs. No one ever got hit by a hamburger again.

And nobody dared to go back to Chewandswallow to find out what had happened to it. They were too afraid."

Henry and I were awake until the very end of Grandpa's story. I remember his good-night kiss.

The next morning we woke up to see snow falling outside our window.

We ran downstairs for breakfast and ate it a little faster than usual so we could go sleddi with Grandpa.

It's funny, but even as we were sliding down the hill we thought we saw a giant pat of butter at the top, and we could almost smell mashed potatoes.

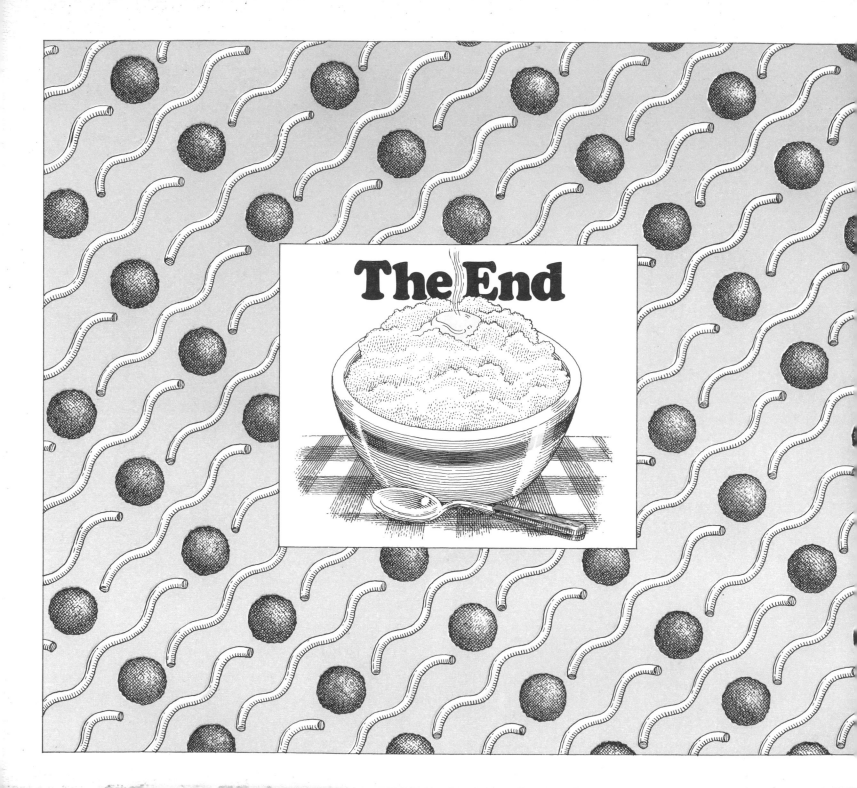

The End